FORGOTTEN TRAILS

PAPER TOWNS: THE GIRL POV

VARTIKA VASHISTA

ISBN 979-888546473-4

I'm grateful for this opportunity to norlights for giving me the chance to write a book. i'd like to thank my family and friends who supported me in this piece of work.

"to those who inspired it, and to those who will not read it."

Contents

Prologue   *vii*

1. Chapter 1   1

2. Chapter 2   3

3. Chapter 3   5

4. Chapter 4   7

5. Chapter 5   10

6. Chapter 6   13

7. Chapter 7   17

8. Chapter 8   21

9. Chapter 9   25

10. Chapter 10   28

11. Chapter 11   31

12. Chapter 12   34

13. Chapter 13   39

14. Chapter 14   42

15. Chapter 15   45

16. Chapter 16   48

17. Chapter 17   52

18. Chapter 18   54

19. Chapter 19   57

20. Chapter 20   59

21. Chapter 21   61

About The Author   63

Prologue

I have always felt like I am a flower in a vase, confined somewhere, looking for a place where it belongs, where it's free. Eventually, the flower dies and is replaced easily, forgotten. But I can't let that happen to me. You can't force something to survive somewhere it doesn't belong to.

I have always been different from others because I believe that's how it should be. I want to mark my own identity, become someone who's different. I want to be remembered. But, the world doesn't have a place for people like me. I don't get along with anyone because they don't understand me. Even my parents don't get me, don't understand what I want with my life. Now, they have stopped caring. They think it's just the rebellious teenager in me, but this is who I am.

You don't always get what you want because you're too comfortable doing what you're doing and don't want things to change.

This world isn't going to give you what you want if you just think it'll change. Because no, it won't, not until you do something for yourself.

He and I were never the same. He was quiet and timid, I was bold and daring. Polar opposites, but somehow I always felt like he was always there for me. He may have not always got me, but he always stood by my side, even when I felt like running away. I'll always love him for the way he was.

I'll be forever grateful that my parents decided to move and I found him.

But right now, I am not where I belong. And I can't pretend I am happy here. I have to find my own world where I can be whoever I want. I am the flower that will pave its own path

and will not be confined anywhere. So I'll have to do it my
way. The Margo way.

ONE

I still remember that tragic day. We were about nine. Our parents were friends so we used to hangout in the Jefferson Park. Quentin biked leaning towards the handlebars, his white sneakers with black detailing a circuitous blur. It was a hot day in March. The sky was clear but the acidic taste in the air felt like it might storm later.

We'd been in the park a lot of times but something felt odd. Even though I couldn't tell right away what was different. I walked forward to figure out whilst Quentin park his bike. "Quentin" I said, in a clam voice, pointing towards something which made it different.

There was an oak tree a few feet in front of me. Thick and crooked and old-looking. But that wasn't different. The playground to our right. Not different either. But now, there was a guy in grey suit, with his back against the trunk. Not moving. I went closer to examine it. Quentin was coming forward with me, I could tell he was scared but he somehow gathered the courage to move closer.

There was blood all over his face and a half-dried blood fountain pouring from his nose. Flies flying over his pale forehead. Mouth half opened in a way that generally shouldn't be.

I couldn't really see Quentin but I could sense taking small steps back. As he moved back, I inched towards him to have a clearer picture. I know he could tell, but I spoke anyway "He's dead". Quentin said nothing. "His eyes are opened" I always thought you close your eyes when you're dead, when all of your strings are broken.

That's what I always thought, people are attached with strings. They get tangled when they're depressed or messed in their head and all untangle when they're happy, and when all of them break, they're dead. People have different beliefs and this was mine.

I kept on going closer to him, until I was close enough to touch his foot. As he kept saying "Margot we gotta go home" "Margot we gotta go home".

"What do you think happened to him?" he stood there but was totally creeped out. "Okay yeah" I said as we ran towards are bikes. It surely was a dreadful experience for Quentin. I could feel his blood rush as he raced his bike. It made me a bit overwhelmed too, I had blood on soles of my shoe. His blood. The dead guy's blood.

As he went home, I went to investigate further as I didn't want to bother Quentin anymore. He already was pretty traumatised, I though. I went to a lot of places asking people if they know him, but all I got was useless information until I went to Mrs. Feldman. She gave me the answers to the questions I was looking for.

TWO

It was about nine o'clock, when I climbed Quentin's window. My face was pressing on his window as I saw his mom tucking him in his bed and turned off the lights and went away. I didn't make any noise, but he noticed me when he turned to his side. He got up and opened the window, but the screen stayed between us. As I made space on the windowsill to sit down, he began with his interrogation, what-I-was-doing-at-his-window and how-I-almost-scared-him-death. But when I told him I did some investigation on that dead guy, he went silent. I took out my little notebook, and a pencil with teeth marks on the eraser, where I wrote the notes. Which I then read to Quentin:

"Mrs. Feldman from over Jefferson court said his name was Robert Joyner. She told me that he lived on Jefferson Road in one of those condos on top of the grocery store, so I went over there are there were a bunch of policemen, and one of them asked if I worked for a school paper, and I said our school didn't have a paper, and he said as long as I wasn't a journalist, he would answer my questions. He said Robert Joyner was thirty-six years old. A lawyer. They wouldn't let me in the apartment, but a lady named Juanita Alverez lives next door to him, and I got into her apartment by asking if I could borrow a cup of sugar, and then she said that Robert Joyner had killed himself with a gun. And the I asked why, and then she told me that he was getting a

divorce and was sad about it."

I paused to flip the notebook page, he was staring deep into my eyes and said "Lots of people get divorces and don't kill themselves" "I know" I said, a tone of excitement in my voice" That's what I said to Juanita Alvarez. And then she said…" I said as I was flipping through my notebook.

"She said that Mr. Joyner was troubled. And then I asked what that meant, and then she told me that we should just pray for him and that I needed to take the sugar to my mom, and I said forget the sugar and left."

He said nothing again. He just looked at me with that little excitement, he was the only person who made me feel important.

"I think I maybe know why," I finally said, breaking the silence.

"Why?"

"Maybe all the strings inside him broke," I said.

As he came forward and placed that screen between us on the floor, but before he could sit back down. I whispered "shut the window." So he did. I didn't leave, just stood there, watching something behind him. He waved at me, smiling. There was something behind him. The dead guy. I don't really remember if that was just an illusion because I was thinking about him the entire day or that was really something. I don't remember how it ended. In my memory, it doesn't end. I keep staring at that still shadow, forever.

I always loved mysteries. And in everything that came after-ward, I could never stop thinking about them that maybe I became one.

THREE

It was a normal school Wednesday morning. I woke on my usual time, took a bit long in the shower, had breakfast and went to school in my silver Honda. It was sometime near prom.

I've been planning something since some time now. And if things go that way, I won't have to attend prom. I didn't like the idea of proms, even though I *had* a boyfriend. Nothing about it was appealing – not slow dancing, not fast dancing, not even the dresses.

But that didn't matter. My best friend, Becca Arrington, and I are pretty popular in high school. My adventure stories would blow through school like a summer storm: an old guy living in a broken-down house in Hot Coffee, Mississippi, taught me how to play guitar. I spent three days traveling with the circus-they thought I had potential on the trapeze. I, who drank a cup of herbal tea with the Mallionaires backstage after the concert in St. Louis while they drank whiskey. I got into that concert by telling the bouncer I was the bassist's girlfriend, and didn't they recognize her, and come o guys seriously my name is Margo Roth Spiegelman and if you go back there and ask the bassist to take a look at me, he'll tell you that I either am his girlfriend or he wishes I was, then the bouncer did so, and then the bassist said "yeah that's my girlfriend let her in the show," and then later she got to *reject the bassist for the Mallionaires.*

The stories, they were shared and were hard to believe, but always proved true. People did hear my stories, but they didn't know me. They didn't know the real Margot Roth Spiegelman, I was that daring person they'd heard about but no one really knew me – what went inside my head. I don't blame others; I am kind of a mysterious person. I liked keeping things secretive. I never really shared anything with my parents, neither did they ever ask. I wasn't close enough to either of them

I was standing in the hallway, next to my locker, beside my boyfriend, Jase. we started dating at the tail end of last year. We're both going university of Florida next year. Jase got a basketball scholarship there. We all were looking Becca Arrington was standing just opposite to me, draped all over this baseball player like she was an ornament and he a Christmas tree. She was my best friend.

My other best friend, Lacey was walking towards me when she saw Becca and tripped over someone in front of her. We burst out laughing. The next class was English, I couldn't resist but kept checking the clock and trying to kill time.

During lunch, while everyone was talking about prom, I was trying to get away from it. Jase asked Lacey "Did you find a date yet?" "Not yet," she shrugged, "but don't worry I soon will". "If you keep rejecting the guys like that, you'll never," said Becca. "She's right, Lacey," said Jase. "Oh, you guys, don't worry about me". With all of the things going on, I couldn't stop thinking about something, something I couldn't get out of my head. While they were talking, something in my head told me it's time for the next adventure. Maybe the a tremendous one.

FOUR

After school, I went straight to Wal-mart and got some black face paint and a black hoodie because it was a chilly evening.

While we were having dinner, mom asked me how my day was, but I was too busy thinking about tonight's errand, I didn't reply to her. Dad started yelling at me for always being such a wuss and always ignoring them. I never liked my parents, all they wanted me to was become like other kids.

But what if I don't want to? What if I want to be different? I knew they'd never support me in something like that. From all the adventures I've ever been to, there were times when I far from home for a couple of days. I left some clues so that my parents or some other people to find where I was. But no one ever did, maybe they never cared or maybe till the time they figured things out I was already home. I'm not really sure which one of these were true. But it didn't matter.

After dinner, while mom and dad were sitting in the living room watching TV, I snuck out and went to Quentin's window wearing black face paint and black hoodie. Q turned around as he heard the window open, staring deep into my eyes were deep green eyes of his. "Are you playing video games?" I asked

"I'm IMing Ben Starling" he said, Ben was his best friend. They were a trio – he, Ben and Radar.

"That doesn't answer my question, perv" he did an awkward laugh and walked over and knelt by the window. I never thought I'd be at his window again; we don't really talk in school too. But here I was.

"To what do I owe this pleasure?" he asked

"I need your car"

"I don't have a car" he shrugged

"Well, I need your mom's car"

"But you've your own car" I puffed my cheeks and sighed "Right, but the thing is my parents have taken away the keys to my car and locked them inside a safe, which they keep under their bed, and Myra Mountweazel" – my who was my dog – "is sleeping in their room. And Myrna Mountweazel has a freaking aneurysm whenever she catches a sight of me. I mean, I could totally sneak in there and steal the safe and crack it and get my keys out and drive away, but the thing is that it's not even worth trying because M is just going to bark like crazy if I so much as I crack open the door. So, like I said, I need a car. Also, I need you to drive it, because I have to do eleven things to do tonight, and at least five of them involve a getaway man"

That wasn't the only reason why I needed him to drive me. I could've asked anyone else to do that, or I could've gone all by myself too. But I've always loved his company and he was the person who'd stick with me till the end, I've always thought. I wanted him to be a rebel and have some fun and to live his life freely – to look at the things differently, find his own point of view for everything, not what the society gives us.

"Any felonies?" he asked

"Hmm" she said "Remind me if we're breaking and entering."

"No," he said, firmly.

"No it's not a felony or no you won't help?"

"No I won't help. Can't you enlist some of your underlings to drive you around. Lacey or Becca? What about Jase, he even has a better car than mine," he said

"They're the part of the problem, actually"

"What's the problem?" he asked

"There are eleven problems" I said a little impatiently "No felonies, I promise" "I swear to god, that you won't be asked to commit any felony"

And exactly then floodlights came all around my house. I rolled under his bed in one swift motion. "Margot" my dad shouted "I saw you!" he was standing in the patio. "oh Christ!" I muffled and got up and went to window. "Come on, dad! I'm just trying to have a chat with Quentin. You're always telling me what a fantastic influence he could have on me and everything"

"Just chatting with Quentin?"

"Yes"

"Then why are you wearing black face paint?"

"Dad, to answer that question would take hours of backstory, and I know you're probably very tired, so just go back t-"

"In the house" he thundered "this minute!"

I grabbed Quentin's shirt and whispered "in a minute!" in his ear, and climbed down the window. Quentin was absolutely clueless for what was going on, honestly, even I wasn't sure.

FIVE

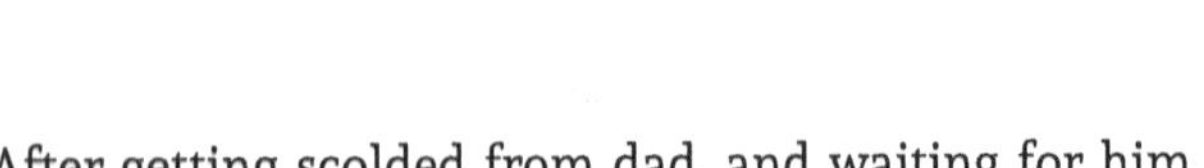

After getting scolded from dad, and waiting for him to go back to his room, I snuck out again. Quentin was standing with key to his minivan. His mom's. I was still wearing that face paint, which had dried out and was a bit irritating.

"I've got school tomorrow" he said

"Yeah, I know" I said "There's school tomorrow and the day after that, and thinking about that for too long can make a girl bonkers. So yeah, it's a school night. That's why we've got to get going, because we've got to be back by morning."

"I don't know."

"Q," I said "Q. darling. How long have we been friends?"

"we're not friends. We're neighbours."

"Oh, Christ, Q. am I not nice to you? Do I not order my various and sundry minions to be kind to you at school?" I used to stop Chuck Parson and his ilk from screwing with them.

"Uh-huh," he answered dubiously

"Q," I said "We have to go."

And so we went. He slid out the window and we ran along side of his house, we opened the doors of the minivan. I whispered not to close the doors – too much noise – so he put it in neutral and pushed off the cement with foot and let it roll down the driveway. We rolled down the street until we switched on the headlights and the engine, and closed the doors. We drove through serpentine streets of Jefferson Park's endlessness. Everything still looking new, like a toy village with dwellings of real people.

"The thing is they don't even care. They just feel like my exploits make them look bad. Just now, do you know what he said? He said 'I don't care if you screw up your life, but don't embarrass us in front of the Jacobsens – they're our friends.' Ridiculous. And you've no idea how hard they've made to get out of the goddamned house. You know how in prison-escape movies they put a pile of clothes under the blanket to make it look like there's a person in there" he nodded. "Yeah, well, mom put a baby monitor in my room so she could hear my sleep-breathing all night. So, I just had to pay Ruthie five bucks to sleep in my room." Ruthie is my little sister "it's *mission: impossible* shit now. Used to be I could sneak out like a regular goddamned American – just climb out the window or jump off the roof. But God, these days, it's like living in a fascist dictatorship."

"Are you going to tell me where we're going?"

"Well, first we're going to Publix. Because of reasons I'll explain later, I need you to go grocery shopping for me. And then to wal-mart."

"What, we're just gonna go on a grand tour of every commercial establishment in Central Florida?" he asked

"Tonight, darling, we're going to right a lot of wrongs. And we're going to wrong some rights. The last shall be first; the meek shall do some earth – inheriting. But before we can radically reshape the world, we need to shop." He pulled into Publix, the parking was almost empty. It was almost midnight.

"Listen," I said, "How much money do you have on you right now?"

"Zero dollars and zero cents," he said while he turned off the engine and looked at me over his shoulder. I wriggled my hand into my pocket and pulled out several hundred-dollar bills.

"Fortunately, the good Lord has provided"

"What the hell?"

"Bat mitzvah money, bitch. I'm not allowed to access the account, but I know my parents' password because they use 'myrnamountw3az31' for everything. So I made a withdrawal" I caught him looking at me, his green eyes staring into mine. It was such a dreamy night, probably the last time seeing him. I smirked "basically," I said, "this is going to be the best night of your life"

SIX

I've to say, with Quentin things are different, I could keep on going on talking with him for two reasons (a) he made me feel like home, I can't describe that feeling, but he always made me seen, unlike other people in school, and (b) it was the only way to avoid silence.

"So right, I made you a list. If you've any questions, just cell my cell. Listen, that reminds me, I took the liberty of putting some supplies in the back of the van earlier."

"What, like, before I agreed to all this?"

"Well yes. Technically yes. Anyway, just call me if you have any questions, but with the Vaseline, you want the one bigger than your fist. There's like a baby Vaseline, then a mommy Vaseline, and then there's a big fat daddy Vaseline, and that's the one you want. If they don't have that, then get, like, three of the mommies." I handed him the list and a hundred-dollar bill and said, "That should cover it."

My list:

cat Fishes – wrapped Separately

Veet (It's for shaving legs Only you don't Need A razor It's with all the Girly cosmetic stuff)

Vaseline

six pack, Mountain Dew

One dozen Tulips

one Bottle Of water

Tissues

one Can of blue spray paint

"Interesting capitalization," he said

"Yeah. I'm a big believer in random capitalization. The rules of capitalization are so unfair to words in the middle." I said. And he went inside the store as I stayed inside the van, my legs placed on the dash board, just waiting for him to come. It was two – thirty in the morning.

"I really don't want to get in any trouble," he said as I used the bottled water and tissues to wipe the black paint off my face. "In my admission letter from the duke it actually explicitly say that they won't take me if I get arrested."

"You're a very anxious person, Q."

"let's just please not get in trouble" he said, "I mean, I want to have fun and everything, but not at an expense of, like, my future."

I looked up, and smiled just the littlest bit. "Its amazes me that you can find all that shit even remotely interesting."

"Huh?"

"College: getting in or no getting in. Trouble: getting or not getting in. School: getting A's or getting D's. Career: having or not having, House: big or small, owning or renting. Money: having or not having. It's all so boring."

He lips moved in a way like he was about to say something, but I just said "Wal-mart."

We entered Wal-mart together and I picked up that thing from the infomercials called The Club, which locks a car's steering wheel into place. As we walked, he asked "Why do we need The Club."

I was still thinking how people are always concerned about this made-up stuff. It should always live-in-the-moment. People are always concerned about their future.

They're always chasing after things, which don't even matter at the moment. I mean, people aren't born into the world to study, get a job, marry, have kids, and die one day. what's the point of life, living this way. There has to be a better way, and I'm gonna find mine.

Ignoring his question, I said "Did you know, that for pretty much the entire history of the human species, the average lifespan was less than thirty years? You could count on ten years or so of real adulthood, right? There's no planning for retirement. There's no planning for career. There's *no planning.* No time for planning. No time for future. Every moment but then the life spans started getting longer, and people started having more and more future, and so they spent more time thinking about it. About the future. And now life has become the future – you get to high school so you can go to college so you can get a good job so you can get a nice house so you afford to send your kids to college so they can get a good job so they can get a nice house so they can afford to send their kids to college"

He didn't really pay attention to what I was saying and repeated "Why do we need The Club?"

I patted his back softly and said, "I mean, obviously this is all going to be revealed to you before the night is over."

While we were getting out of the store, I took out my air horn. "No." "No, what?" I said.

"No, don't blow the h-" before he could finish, I started blowing the horn.

"I'm sorry I couldn't here you. What was that?" I said

"Stop b-" I started blowing the horn again.

A wal-mart employee came over to me, almost our age, and said "Hey, you can't use your horn here,"

"I'm sorry, I didn't know that"

"Oh it's cool," he said, "I don't mind, actually."

He couldn't stop staring at me. And asked, "What are you guys up to tonight?"

"Nothing much, you?"

"I get off at one and then I'm going out ot this bar down on Orange, if you want to come. But you'd have to drop off your brother, they're really strict about IDs."

Quentin got a little mad at him calling Q my brother, and said, "I'm not her brother," looking at the guy's sneakers.

"Yeah, he's my cousin actually," I said, continuing lying. I put my hand around his waist, and added "and my lover."

He rolled his eyes and went back. As my hand was still lingering around his waist, he put his around mine. I could feel his fingers on against my waist.

"You really are my favourite cousin," he said. I smiled at him and bumped him softly, and spun away.

"don't I know it," I said.

SEVEN

It was 1:07. He was driving following my directions. He was happy, I could tell that. That spark in his eyes, it wasn't something usual. It was rare. I turned away from him, staring out of the window, smiling, I said "Isn't it pretty, huh?"

"I love driving fast under the streetlights" he said, still looking forward.

"Light," he said, "The visible reminder of Invisible Light."

"It's beautiful," I said.

"T.S. Eliot" he said. "You read it too, last year in English"

"Oh, it's a quote," I said, a bit dispirited way. I've always been a fan of literature. That's one of the things a lot of people don't know about. Not even Quentin. But that quote, to me it means that light is just a reminder of the everything we don't have. There are many things we perceive but there are many more things we don't have or maybe can't have. Nevertheless, they exist. And these visible things serve as a reminder of those invisible. There is more to the world than we can think of. It remined me of things I couldn't have. But, because of them, I became the rebel I am today. It still pains, thinking about them.

"Say it again," I said.

"Light, the visible reminder of invisible light."

"Yeah. Damn, that's good. That must help with your lady friend."

"Ex-lady friend," he corrected me.

"Suzie dumped you?" I asked

"How do you know *she* dumped *me*?"

"Oh, sorry"

"Although she did," he admitted, and I laughed. I didn't really know about them, I actually didn't pay attention to school-drama much. It was Lacy who sometimes updated me about stuff. But that's pretty much it.

I put my feet on the dash board and said, "Right, well, I'm sorry to hear that. But I can relate. My lovely boyfriend these many months is messing with my best friend."

He looked over, "Seriously?"

I stayed silent, watching the buildings pass by, everything was so peaceful.

"But you were just laughing with him this morning, I saw you."

"I don't know what you're talking about. I heard it before the lunch period, and then found them both talking together and I started screaming bloody murder, and Becca ran into the arms of Clint Bauer, and Jase was just standing there like a dumbass with the chaw drool running out his stank mouth."

"that's weird, because Chuck Parson asked me this morning what I knew about Jase and you."

"Yeah, well, Chuck does as he's told, I guess. Probably trying to find out for Jase who knew."

"Jesus, why would Jase fool around with Becca?"

"Well, she's not known personality or generosity of spirit, so it's probably because she's hot"

"She's not as hot as you"

I turned towards him, "That's always seemed so ridiculous to me, that people would want to be around because they're pretty. It's like picking breakfast cereal based on color instead of taste. It's the next exit, by the way. But I'm not pretty, not close up anyway. Generally, the closer people get to me the less hot they"

"That's-"

"Whatever." I cut him off. I didn't want him to continue. Opinions differ, it doesn't make sense to me though, how people are so caught in things like this. We don't choose how we look, I've always thought how unfair it is to judge people on things they can't control. If you really want to judge people, judge them for something they did. How they chose to put it the way they did, not for something the universe gave them.

I watched him go silent, eyes still on the road, still looking forward. I tilt my head towards the window, looking at the streetlights as we passed by them.

"Becca does sort of suck," he said, breaking the silence.

"Yeah," still looking outside.

"Well, this'll be fun at any rate," I said, as I took out The Club of the bag.

"Where are we going?"

"Becca's"

"Uh-oh" he said, and started to pull up to some sign, I couldn't really see. He parked the minivan and started telling me that she's taking me home.

"No felonies, promise! We need to find Jase's car. Becca's street is the next one up on the right, he wouldn't park his car on her street, because her parents are home. Try the one after. That's the first thing."

"Ok," he said, "But after that we go home."

"No, then we move on to part two of eleven."

“Margo, that's a bad idea.”
“Just drive” and so he did.

EIGHT

Jase's Lexus was two blocks down Becca's street.

I jumped out of the minivan, even before he could bring it to complete stop, but I was so thrilled, I couldn't hold it.

I climbed back inside to take the keys to The Club, "Dummy never locks his car."

I reached over and tousled his hair and said, "Part one – done. Now, to Becca's"

I explained him part two and three to him as he drove. "Well, after what he did to you, he kind of deserves this" he said, not sounding too agreed. He didn't mean that, he was drowning with nervousness. I glanced at him, and turned again, nodding.

As he turned on to Becca's Street, I crawled to the back of the minivan and dug through all the stuff we had there. I returned with a pair of binoculars and a digital camera. I looked through the binoculars, light on in the basement but no movement. I handed them to Quentin. He looked through them and then took out his cell. He dialled the number, I recited to him.

"Mr. Arrington," he asked. I wanted him to call as no one would recognise his voice. I waited, still excited. But at the same time, I was mad at Jase cheating on me, not because I loved him, but because he was my boyfriend – he isn't supposed to do all that stuff.

"Sir, I think you should know that your daughter is currently in the basement with Jason Worthington," and he hung up. Part two: accomplished.

I and Quentin climbed inside the minivan and charged down the street after running in Becca's yard. I gave him the camera and we waited for the bedroom lights to come on, and then straight light, kitchen light, and then finally stairway down to the basement.

"Here he comes," I whispered. As he wiggled out of the basement window, Quentin jumped and took a picture of him. I tugged onto hi leg. He looked at me and I passed him a goofy smile. He, then, helped me get up and we raced back to the car. As he was starting the engine, I said "Let me see the picture."

He handed me the camera, my fingers against his and our heads almost touching. Looking at Jase's pale face, Quentin laughed "Oh, god" I giggled, looking at the picture.

"We've to go," I said "the basement."

"What? why?"

"Part five"

"No."

"Yes. Now." I said, "She's upstairs, getting yelled at by her parents. But, like, how long does it last? I mean, what do you say? 'You shouldn't screw Margo's boyfriend in the basement.' It's basically one-sentence lecture. So we need to hurry."

He didn't say anything just gave me an annoyed look, but I knew he's going to come along anyway.

I got out of the car with a spray paint in one hand and the fish in other, and he whispered "This is a bad idea," but followed behind me. The basement window was still opened, that means she's still upstairs. "I'll go first," I said. I climbed the window and stood on Becca's desk, half inside the house and half out of it.

"Can't I just lookout?" he asked.

"Get your skinny ass here," I answered, and he got inside. After checking out the basement, he turned towards me and I handed him the wrapped catfish and one of Becca's glittered lavender pen. I told him what to write-

A message from Margo Roth Spiegelman: Your friendship with her – it sleeps with fishes.

And I hid the fish between her clothes, in her closet. As I was facing the closet, I could hear the footsteps. As they got a little loud, Quentin tapped my shoulder. I turned and smiled and pulled out the spray paint. I shook the bottle and painted the letter M onto the wall above the desk. I reached for Quentin, and he pulled me through the window. As I was starting to stand, we heard someone shout "DWIGHT!". We took off running, Quentin ahead of me.

I turned around, still running, the front door Becca's house opened, and heard a high – pitched voice shout "HALT!" and heard a shotgun being pumped. "Gun," I whispered. I couldn't really figure out who it was, but I think it was Jase.

We were just one block away from the minivan, and Quentin – instead of running around the hedge – he leaped over it head first. He didn't land right, instead he tried to do a summersault, but ended up head over heels on the road.

I pulled him up, and then we were in the car. He was driving in reverse with headlights off. Jase was fast, he was running at us. But he wasn't running at any particular place. I don't think if he saw either of us, he didn't recognise the minivan too for two reasons (a) Quentin never drove the van to school (b) I didn't hang out with Quentin in school, never really. Not because I was embarrassed or something, but I hardly ever saw him in the hallway, and our friends didn't get along very well.

NINE

He turned on the lights, driving forward now.

"I kinda felt bad for him," he said, in a low voice because he knew it'll annoy me. And it did.

"For him? Why? Because he's been cheating on me for six weeks? Because he's a disgusting idiot who will probably be rich and happy his whole life, thus proving the absolute unfairness of the cosmos?"

"He just looked sort of desperate," he said.

"Whatever. We're going to Karin's house. It's on Pennsylvania, by ABC Liquors."

"Don't be pissed at me," he said. "I just had a pointing a freaking shotgun at me for helping you, so don't be pissed at me."

"I'M NOT PISSED AT YOU!" I shouted, and punched the dashboard.

"Well, you're screaming."

"I thought maybe – whatever. I thought maybe, he wasn't cheating."

"Oh."

"Karin told me at school. And I guess a lot of people have known for a long time. And no one told me until Karin. And I thought maybe she was just trying to stir up drama or something."

"I'm sorry," he said.

"Yeah, yeah. I can't even believe I even care."

"My heart is really pounding"

"That's how you know, you're having fun," I said, glancing over him.

It really was fun. And I know, even if he doesn't admit, he did have fun. As much as he loved to stay at home and worry about that made – up shit, I loved to make him feel alive, maybe that was the list night I'm seeing him. Even though, I wanted to last forever, I knew it couldn't. That's why I chose him to come with me, so he could really get out of what the society fits in the heads of people and think for himself. I didn't want him to spend the rest of his life living in those closed spaces and worrying out. Because he was the only person who actually cared about me, I couldn't just leave him the way it was. It was also a way of me saying him goodbye.

"My pulse is dangerously high," he said, totally freaked out.

"I don't even remember the last time I got excited about something like that. The adrenaline in the throat and the lungs expanding"

"In through the nose out through the mouth," he answered me

"All your little anxieties. It's just so…"

"Cute?"

"Is that what they're calling childish these days?" I smiled.

I crawled backseat, and dug through the stuff – got out a nail paint bottle. "While you calm down, I'm going to paint my nails."

"You just take your time," he said, looking at me through the mirror and smiled.

And so I crawled back to the front seat. My nail paint balanced on the dashboard and me staring out the window.

TEN

"Part six," I said, "Leave flowers and an apologetic note."

"Why'd you do to her?"

"Well, when she told me about the Jase, I sort of shot the messenger."

"How so?" he asked. A bunch of kids in a sports car were next to us – revving their engine. As if asking us to race the Chrysler.

"Well, I don't remember exactly what I called her, but it something along the lines of snivelling, repulsive, idiotic, brackenridge, snaggletooth, fat-ass bitch with the worst hair in Central Florida – and that's saying something."

"Her hair *is* ridiculous," he said.

"I *know*. That was the only thing I said about her that was true. When you say nasty things about people, you should never say the true ones, because you can't really fully and honestly take those back, you know? I mean, there are highlights. And there are streaks. And then there are skunk stripes."

I went back again, as he reached Karin's house and returned with a bouquet of white tulips. A note was taped to one of the stems of the flowers, folded like an envelope. Once the car was stopped, I gave Quentin the bouquet and he went down the sidewalk and placed the flowers on Karin's doorstep and sprinted back.

"Part seven," I said, as soon as he got inside the minivan. "Leave a fish for the lovely Mr. Worthington."

"I suspect he won't be home yet," he said, with a hint of pity of his voice.

"I hope the cop finds him barefoot and frenzied in some roadside ditch a week from now," I said, pretty discourteously.

"Remind me never to cross Margo Roth Spiegelman," he mumbled, and I laughed.

"Seriously," I said "We bring the freaking rain down on our enemies."

"Your enemies," he corrected.

"We'll see," I answer, and then perked up and said, "Oh, hey, I'll handle this one. The thing about Jason's house is they have crazy good security system. And we can't have another panic attack."

"Umm," he said.

He lived not long from Karin's, in this *rich* subdivision called Casavilla. Jason's dad built all the houses in that division. All Spanish – style, with red roof tiles and all. He's one of the richest land developers in Florida, "Big, ugly homes for bis, ugly people," Quentin said as we pulled into Casavila.

"No shit. If I ever end up being the kind of people who has one kid and seven bedrooms, do me a favour and shoot me." I said, jokingly.

We pulled up to Jase's house and I grabbed the catfish and uncapped a pen with my teeth, and scribbled in a different handwriting:

MS's love For you: it Sleeps With the Fishes

"Listen, keep the car on," I said

"Okay," he replied.

"Keep it in drive."

"Okay," he said, but seemed dispassionate.

With catfish in one hand and spray paint in another, I loped across their lawn and hid behind an oak tree. I waved at Quentin from the darkness, thought he won't really see me, it was really dark, but he waved back. Then I took a deep breath – my cheeks puffed – exhaled, turned around and ran. I had just taken a step when the siren started going off and the house lit up with a million lights, I knew this would happen and came prepared, I heaved the fish through the window, the sirens were too loud too hear the glass breaking. Then I took time, and carefully spray painted the letter M on the unshattered part of the window. I ran straight to the car, and jumped into the car and we were gone even before I could close the door. He stopped at the stop sign and I said "What the hell? Go, go, go!" and he said "Oh, right." We rolled through the three signs in Casavila, and were a mile down Pennsylvania Avenue before we saw a cop car roar past us.

"That was pretty hardcore," I said. "I mean, even for me. To put it Q – style, my pulse is a little elevated."

"Jesus," he said, "I mean, you couldn't have just left it in his car? Or his doorstep?"

"We bring the freaking rain, Q. not the scattered showers."

ELEVEN

"Tell me the part eight is less terrifying," He said, tilting is head towards mine and looking at me.

"Don't worry. Part eight is a child's play. We're going back to Jefferson Park. Lacey's house. You know where she lives right?" he did. She lived opposite to the Jefferson Park, a mile away from ours – the same block where the dead guy had lived on, actually. I'd been to her place a million times before. There were two locked doors when you get into the condo. And to everyone's surprise, even I didn't know what was in there. Even I couldn't break into those. Maybe because of privacy reasons of people who lived there or people who live beside those locked doors, I'm not sure why.

"So has Lacey been naughty or nice?" he asked, turning towards me.

"Lacey has been distinctly naughty," I said, gawking.

"I mean, we have been friends since kindergarten."

"And?"

"And she didn't tell me about Jase. But not just that. When I look back on it, she's just a *terrible* friend. I mean, for instance, do you think I'm fat?"

"Jesus, no," he said. "You're –" he stopped.

"You shouldn't lose any weight." He said.

I laughed, waving my hand at him. He glanced at me, and passed a wacky look, we joked and laughed until my eyes watered. As I was wiping my tears from all those laughs, I caught him gawking at me. The stillness in his eyes, not just the green color of his eyes, there was something else which enchanting about it. The Quentin – ness they had. Those deep green charming eyes – perfection.

"But she would always make these little comments," I said "I'd loan you these shorts but I don't think they'd fit right on you.' Or, 'You're so spunky. I love how you just make guys fall in love with your personality.' Constantly undermining me. I don't think she ever said anything that wasn't an attempt at undermination."

"Undermining."

"Thank you, Annoying McMasterGrammician."

"Grammarian," he corrected, again.

"Oh my God, I'm going to kill you!" I said, laughing.

We drove along the edges of the Park, to avoid driving in front of the houses. Just in case our parents have discovered our disappearance. We passed through the lake, then turned onto the Jefferson Court, and then drove onto the little faux downtown. We stopped a block away, in the first parking spot we found not under the streetlight.

"Would you please hand me the last fish?" I asked.

It had already been started to smell bad, so we were glad it was the last one. And then I wrote on the paper wrapper positioning it on the dashboard:

your Friendship Sleeps with The fishes.

We mould our way through the glow of lights, walking as free and easy as two friends can when one of them was carrying a fish in a wrapper and the other one was holding a can of blue spray paint. A dog started to bark, we could do nothing but stood where we were, frozen. It went quite again. But he could smell the fish probably. We went forward, step – by – step, s quietly as we could. And we made it to Lacey's car. It was locked.

"Well, that makes it harder," I said as reached into my pocket and pulled out a length of wire that had once been a coat hanger. I unlocked her car with that wire. Quentin was amazed by my weird skill, I laughed.

I got inside the car from the driver's side and asked him to help me opening the other side. Then we pulled the backseat up together. I slipped the fish underneath it, and then we slammed the seat down on the fish on the count of three. The sound of catfish being exploded was disgusting. The way her SUV would smell after just a few hours, I'll admit the kind of serenity washed over me.

"Put an M on the roof for me," I said. He nodded without thinking twice and climbed the back bumper of the car. He lettered an M in one swift motion and jumped off the car. He held his blue fingertips for me to see, and I smiled and held his against my blue fingertips. And as Quentin would say, my pulse went high.

"Part nine – done," I said.

TWELVE

It was 2:49 in the morning. I was laying back on the passenger seat, still staring outside. I rolled down the window. Fascinated by the empty roads and peace and light breeze blowing against my face brushing my light brown hair back, warmer that night. And all the city lights. I've always loved the night life. Alone, among all the tall buildings. This whole and amazing and endless world, mine for exploring.

Quentin, following my directions, said "You just giving me the tour?"

"No," I said "That's on South." We drove for another four blocks and turned. I pointed, smiling, and there, in front of us, wad the Asparagus.

The asparagus is just a sculpture that bears an uncanny resemblance to thirty – foot – tall piece of asparagus.

It does *not* look like a Tower of light, at any rate, which is the actual name of the sculpture. Quentin pulled into the parking lot and looked over me, I was staring at the middle distance just for a moment. I wasn't looking at the building, but past it.

"May I ask why you have taken me to the Asparagus?" he said.

I turned towards him and passed a fake smile.

"We gotta check on our progress. And the best place to do that is from the top of the SunTrust Building."

He rolled his eyes. "Nope. No. No way. You said no breaking and entering."

"This isn't breaking and entering. It's just entering, because there's an unlocked door."

"Margo that's ridiculous. Of c –"

"As I've acknowledged that over the course of the evening there has been both breaking and entering. There was entering at Becca's house. There was breaking at Jase's. and there will be entering here. But there has never been simultaneously breaking and entering. Theoretically, the cops could charge us with breaking, and they could charge us for entering. But they couldn't charge us for breaking *and* entering. So, I've kept my promise."

"Surely, the SunTrust building has a security guard or something."

"Of course," I said, unbuckling my belt "They do, his name is Gus."

As we walked inside, a young guy with a goatee was standing behind a semi-circular table, wearing a security uniform.

"What's up Margo?" he said

"Hey Gus!" I said.

"Who's the kid?" he asked.

"This is my colleague, Q. Q, this is Gus." Quentin seemed annoyed on being called a kid, but didn't say anything.

"What's up Q?" asked Gus.

"Not much," he said.

"Elevators are down for the night," Gus said, "Had to shut 'em them off at three, you're welcome to use the stairs though."

"Cool! See ya, Gus"

"See ya Margo"

"How the hell do you know the security guard at the SunTrust building?" he asked at we turned, and were walking towards the stairs.

"He was a senior when we were Freshmen," I answered. "We gotta hustle, okay? Time's watching." I tried to take two stairs at a time, trying to get there quicker. Quentin was behind me, trying to walk faster. But couldn't catch up, and I didn't wait for him. When he reached the twenty – fifth floor, I was already standing on the landing, waiting for him.

"Check it out" I said, as I opened a stairwell door towards a huge room with an oak table long enough to fit two whole cars on top of it, and a long window – from floor to the ceiling.

"Conference room," I said "It's got the best view in the whole building."

I walked along the windows and he followed me.

"Okay so there," pointing, "is Jefferson Park. See our houses? Lights still off, so that's good." I walked a few steps. "Jase's house. Lights off, no more cop cars. Excellent, although it might mean he's made it home, which is unfortunate." Becca's house was too far to see, even from up here.

I stood silent for a while and then walked right to a pane and leaned my forehead against glass. Quentin stayed back, but I pulled him forward by his T – shirt.

From here, Orlando looked magical. The skyline perfectly lit. The calm surroundings. The view was just so mesmerising. The streets were desolate. The storefronts were devoid of displays, which was just as well, because not a single person was there to admire them. Cars sat empty along the curb, collecting dust.

The streetlamps that weren't burned out projected little circles of white light onto an empty, cracked sidewalk. The traffic light swung in the breeze, telling all the non-existent drivers to stop. The 'walk' sign was on, letting all the non-existent pedestrians step out onto the faded white lines of the crosswalk.

"It's beautiful," he said.

"Really? You think so?" I scoffed

"I mean, well, maybe not," he said, although we both knew it *was*.

We could see it all; there was school. There was Jefferson Park. There, at a distance, Disney World. There was the 7-Eleven where I painted my nails and he fought for breath. It was here – our whole world, just from a building.

"It's more impressive," he said, in an excited tone, "From, a distance, I mean. You can't see the wear on things, you know? You don't see the rust or the weeds or the paint cracking. You see the place as someone once imagined it."

"Everything's uglier close up," I added.

"Not you," he said, I smiled, still leaning on the glass. "Here's a tip: you're cute when you're confident. And less when you're not."

Before he could continue, I turned towards the glass again. "here's what's not beautiful about it: from here you can't see the rust or the crackling of the pain or whatever, but you can tell what the place really is. You see how fake it is. It's not even hard enough to be made out of plastic. It's a paper town. I mean look at it, Q. Look at all those streets that turn on themselves. All the houses that were built to fall apart. All those paper people living in those paper houses. Burning the future to stay warm. Everyone demented with the mania of owning things. All the things paper thin and paper frail. And all the people, too." I said. I've lived here for eighteen years, and never have I ever once in my life come across anyone who cares about anything that matters.

"I'll try not to take that personally," Quentin said. We were both staring at an inky – distance and soon both sank into that ink.

THIRTEEN

We were in the minivan, the engine not stared yet. "What time do your parent's usually wake – up, by the way?"

"I don't know, like six-fifteen." It was 3:51. "I mean, we have two-plus hours and we're through with nine parts."

"I know, and I've saved the most libations one for the last. Anyway, we'll get it all done. Part ten – Q's turn to pick a victim."

"What?"

"I've already picked the punishment. Now you gotta pick who we're going to rain our mighty wrath down on."

"Upon whom we are going to rain our mighty wrath," he corrected and shook my head. "And I don't really have anyone upon whom I want to rain down my wrath."

"What about Chuck?" I asked.

"Hmm," he said.

Chuck parson was a horrible person. Apart from being a cafeteria conveyor belt debacle, he once grabbed Q outside the school while he was waiting for the bus and twisted his arm and kept saying, "Call yourself a faggot."

Which, in the end, he had to. Chuck Parson was no Aristotle when it came to logic. But he was 270 pounds and six – three, which clearly, counts for something."

"You can make a case for Chuck." He admitted. And turned towards the wheel and made his way back to the interstate.

"Remember at the crown school of dance?" I asked "I was just thinking about tonight."

"Ugh. Yeah."

"I'm sorry about that, by the way. I've no idea went with him."

"Yeah, it's all good" he said. I kind of sensed it wasn't, but didn't say anything. "Yeah. Chuck Parson. You know where he lives?" he asked.

"I know I could bring out your vengeful side" I said, smirking. "He's in College Park. Get off at Princeton." He turned onto the interstate entrance ramp. "Woah there," I said. "Don't break the Chrysler."

In the sixth grade, a bunch of kids including me and Chuck and Quentin were forced by our parents to take ballroom dance lessons at the Crown School of Humiliation, Degradation and Dance. Girls would stand on one side and boys on the other. And when the teacher told them to, the boys would walk over to the girls and say "May I have this dance?" with one hand behind their back and other offering to the girl, and the legs crossed – one behind the other. And the girl would say "You may." Girls weren't allowed to say no. Then one day, when we were doing the fox-trot. Chuck convinced everyone to say no to Q. So he went to this girl – Mary Beth and said "May I have a dance?" and she said no. Then he went to another girl who also said no. He, then, came over to me, and even I said no. And then another, and then he started to cry.

Crying at the rejection was worse than getting rejected at the dance school, and the only thing worse was going up to the teacher and saying in tears "The girls are saying no, but they are not *supposedtuh*."

So long story short, Chuck made middle school and fox-trot embarrassing enough for Quentin, that *he* wasn't going to lament his suffering anymore.

"Wait, he won't know it's me, will he?"

"Nope, why?"

"I don't want him to think I give enough shit about him to hurt him." He put his hand down on the centre console.

"don't worry" I patted his hand." He'll never know what depilated him."

"I think you misused a word, but I'm not sure what it means"

"I know a word you don't know," I chanted. "I'M THE NEW QUEEN OF VOCABULARY! I'VE USURPED YOU!"

"Spell *usurped*," he said.

"No," I answered laughing "I'm not giving you my crown over *usurped*. You'll have to do it better."

"Fine," he smiled.

FOURTEEN

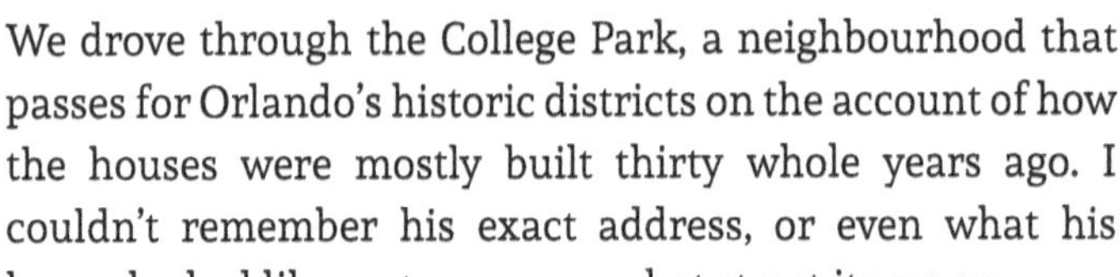

We drove through the College Park, a neighbourhood that passes for Orlando's historic districts on the account of how the houses were mostly built thirty whole years ago. I couldn't remember his exact address, or even what his house looked like, not even sure what street it was on.

After passing through three blocks of Vassar Street, I pointed to my left and said, "That one!"

"Are you sure?"

"I'm like ninety – seven – point – two percent sure. I mean, I'm pretty sure his bedroom is right there," pointing. "One time he had a party, and when the cops came shimmied out his bedroom window."

"It seems like we could get in trouble."

"But if the window's opened there's no breaking involved. Only the entering. And we just did entering at that SunTrust building, and it wasn't that big of a deal, right?"

He laughed and said "You're turning me into a badass."

"That's the idea," I winked. "Okay, supplies: get the Veet, the spray paint, and the Vaseline."

"Okay." And he grabbed all the stuff.

"Now don't freak me out, Q. the good news is Chuck sleeps like a hibernating bear – I know because I had English with him last year and he wouldn't wake up even when Ms. Johnstonswatted him with Jane Eyre. So we're going to go up to his bedroom window, we're gonna open it, we're gonna take off our shoes, and then very quietly go inside, and I'm going to screw with Chuck. Then you and I are going to screw with Chuck. Then you and I are going to fan out to opposite sides of the house, we're going to cover every single door handle in Vaseline, so if someone wakes up, they'll have hella hard time to catch us. Then we'll screw with Chuck some more, paint his house a little, and we're outta there. And no talking."

We walked away from the car together when I reached down for his hand, entangle my fingers between his', and squeezed. He squeezed back and glanced at me. I nodded, and he nodded back, and then I let go of his hand. We gently scampered the window. He pushed the wooden casing up, trying to make no noise at all. It squeaked a little but opened in one swift motion. It was dark inside, but we could see the bed, and Chuck lying on the bed.

The window was a bit high, so Quentin put his hands together and I stepped a socked foot onto his hands and he uplifted me. My entrance was as silent as grave, it would've made a ninja jealous. He then jumped inside, in the most complicated way possible. It was all quite until I heard him groan and turned around to check, he hit himself against the windowsill.

His nightstand light came on. Some old guy – decidedly not Chuck Parson – was laying in bed. With eyes wide awake in terror and didn't say a word.

"Umm," I said. "Um, I think we've the wrong house." I turned around and wanted to run away from there. But Quentin stood there, like an idiot, blocking my exit. I looked at him urgently, and he realised what he was doing. We grabbed our shoes and took off.

We got inside the minivan, and he barrelled the car. Soon we were on the other street, and slowed it a little.

FIFTEEN

After sometime, still in the minivan, I said "I think we share the blame on this one."

"Um, you picked the wrong house," he shrugged.

"Right, but you're the one who made noise." He said nothing. We drove in circles for some time. After a few minutes, he finally said, "We could probably get his address off internet. Radar has a log-in to the school dictionary."

"Brilliant."

He called Radar, but it straight went to voice mail. He could try his home phone, but his parent's where friends with his', so that wouldn't work. Then, he finally called Ben. He wasn't Radar, but knew all of his passwords. It went to voice mail, but after ringing. So he called again. Voice mail. He called again. Voice main, again.

"He obviously isn't answering," I said, but he dialled again anyway.

"Oh, he'll answer," he said. After a few more calls, he did.

"I need you to use Radar's login to the student dictionary and look up an address. Chuck Parson."

"No." Ben said.

"Please," he said.

"No."

"You'll be glad you did this, Ben. I promise."

"Yeah, yeah. I just did it. I was doing it while saying no – can't help but help. Four – two – two Amherst. Hey, why do you want Chuck Parson's address at four-twelve in the morning?"

"Get some sleep, Benners."

"I'm going to assume this was a dream," and he hung up.

It was only a few blocks down. We reached in almost no time, parked at street 418, picked our supplies and jogged across his lawn. It was almost morning, dew shaking off grass as we ran along the fence.

His window was lower than that old guy, we climbed anyway. Quentin went first and pull me up. I tiptoed to Chuck, and Quentin stood behind me. I pulled out the Veet, sprayed some on my palm, and carefully spread some on his right eyebrow. He didn't so much as twitch.

Then I carefully opened the Vaseline – the lid made a loud *clorp*. We immediately checked out Chuck – just to see if he woke up or anything. He showed no sign of waking. I scooped a big gob of it into my hand, and we headed off to opposite sides of the house. I, then, slathered Vaseline on his bedroom door, and then silently opened his parent's bedroom and Vaseline the inner knob – with the slightest creak – shut the door. I went straight to his bedroom; Quentin was there after a few seconds too. We slathered every part of his window with the leftover Vaseline, we didn't close it – thinking it'll be harder to open.

I glanced at my watch and held up two fingers. And we waited. We just stood there, staring at each other, for those two minutes. I watched his green eyes, hardly even blinking. No one said nothing, just stood silently, drowning into that magical moment. It was nice – in the dark and quiet. The way his eyes looked back at mine, it felt like – there was something worth seeing.

I nodded, then we walked over to Chuck. Q wrapped his hand around his t-shirt, as I'd told him. He leaned forward, softly and gently wiping the Veet off. With it came every last hair that had been on his right eyebrow. He was leaning over Chuck Parson, with his T-shirt above his eyebrow, when he's eyes shot opened. Lightening flash, I grabbed his comforter and threw it at him. Before he could figure things out or even shout for help, I jumped out of the window. Quentin followed. Chuck started screaming, but only after we were out, "MOM! DAD! ROBERY! ROBERY!"

The only thing these robbers stole was his right eyebrow. I swung out of the window and carefully landed. I got up and started to spray paint letter M onyo the vinyl siding of Chuck's house. As I was in the middle of lettering, Quentin landed on me. We grabbed our shoes and rushed to the minivan. I turned back to check, the lights were on but no one outside, a testament to the brilliant simplicity of the well-Vaselines doorknobs. We then drove in reverse, to the Princeton Street and then to interstate.

SIXTEEN

"Did you see it? His face without the eyebrow? He looks like permanently doubtful, you know? Like, 'oh, really? You're saying I've only one eyebrow?' like story. And I love making that jerk choose: better to shave off Lefty, or paint on the Righty. Oh, I just love it, how he yelled for his mama" I said. We were still talking about Chuck.

"Wait, why do you hate him?" he asked.

"I didn't say I hate him. I said he was a jerk."

"But you were you always kinda friends with him," he said. That's because he used to be friend's with him. And he being the bully he was, it was kind of a perk having him around – I asked him not to screw Q too, and a bunch of my other friends. Not like I liked him, but at least he would listen to me.

"Yeah, well, I was always kinda friends with a lot of people," I said. I leaned towards the seat and rested on head on his shoulder, and said, "I'm tired."

"Caffeine," he said. And I turned back and looked for Mountain Dew. I passed it to him and he drank it in long chugs.

"So, we're going to Sea World," I told him. "Part eleven." I couldn't believe it was the final part. It was near the end – so soon.

"What, are we going to free willy or something?"

"No," I said. "We're just going to go to Sea World, that's it. It's just a theme park I haven't broken into yet."

"We can't break into the Sea World," he said as he pulled over into some parking lot of a store and turned off the car.

"We're in a bit of time crunch," I said, and leaned over him to start the car again. He pushed my hand and said, "We can't break into Sea World," he repeated.

"There you go with the breaking again," I opened a Mountain Dew, and a car passed us at the very moment, its lights flashed at our faces, I could see him staring at me as I glanced over him from the corner of my eyes, still drinking Mountain Dew. And got almost prepared to give that lecture all over again. "We're not going to *break* anything. Don't think of it as breaking it into Sea World. Think of it as visiting the Sea World in the middle of the night for free."

"Well, first off, we'll get caught," he said.

"Off course, we'll get caught. So what?" I said. The car still in the parking lot.

"So what?" He totally freaked out now, "it's illegal."

"Q, in the scheme of things, what kind of trouble can Sea World put us in? I mean, Jesus, everything I've done for you, you can't do this for me? You can't just shut up and calm down and stop being so goddamned terrified of every little adventure?" then I said, under my breath, "I mean, god, grow some nuts."

He got mad. He unbuckled his seatbelt and turned towards me and said "after everything YOU'VE done for ME?" almost screaming. "Did you call MY friend's father who was screwing MY boyfriend so on one would know that I was calling? Did you chauffeur MY ass all around the world not because you're oh-so-important to me but because I needed a ride and you were close by? Is that kinda shit you've done for me tonight?"

I was staring outside the entire time. At the vinyl siding od the furniture store. "You think I needed you? You don't think i could have given Myrna Mountweazel a Benadryl so she'd sleep through my stealing the safe from under my parents' bed? Or snuck into your bedroom while you were sleeping and taken your car key? I didn't need you, you idiot. I *picked* you. And then you picked me back." Now I looked at him. "And that's like a promise. At least for tonight. In sickness and health. In good times and in bad. For richer, for poorer. Till dawn do us part."

He started the car and we got off the parking lot. He finally said, "Fine, but when Sea World, Incorporated or whatever sends a letter to Duke University saying miscreant Quinten Jacobsen broke into their facility at four thirty in the morning with a wide-eyed lass at his side, Duke University will be mad. Also, my parents will be mad."

"Q, you're going to Duke. You're going to be a very successful layer-or-something and get married and have babies and live your whole life whole life and then die one day. And in your last moments, when you're choking on your own bile in the nursing home, you'll say to yourself: 'Well, I wasted my whole goddamned life, but at least I broke into the Sea World with Margo Roth Spiegelman my senior year of high school. At least I carpe'd that one diem.'"

"*Noctem*," he corrected.

"Okay, you're the grammar king again. You've regained your throne. Now take me to Sea World."

We silently drove for a few blocks. "Margo," he said, breaking the silence.

"Q."

"You said... when that guy died, you said maybe all the strings inside him broke, and then you just said that about yourself, and that last string broke."

I giggled. "You worry too much. I don't want some kids to find me swarmed with flies on a Saturday morning in Jefferson Park." I waited for a second for the punch line, "I'm too vain for the fate."

He laughed and was relieved. We exited the interstate, and turned to the International Drive, the tourism capital of the world. There were innumerable shops on the International Drive, and all of them sold things made out of crap. Crap moulded into seashells, key rings, refrigerator magnets, whatever.

But at 4:50 in the morning, the tourists were sleeping. The drive was completely dead. We drove past the store after parking lot after store after parking lot.

"Sea World is just past the parkway," I said, I went to the backseat again, digging into the backpack, again.

"I got all these satellite maps and drew our plan of attack, but I can't freaking find them anywhere. But any just go right past the parkway, and on our left there will be this souvenir shop."

"On my left, there are about seventeen thousand souvenir shop."

"right, buy there'll only be one on the right after the parkway."

And there was one. He pulled into an empty parking lot and parked the car directly beneath a streetlight, because cars are generally getting stolen on 1-Drive. And since it wasn't Quentin car - it was his mom's, we couldn't afford to get it stolen.

SEVENTEEN

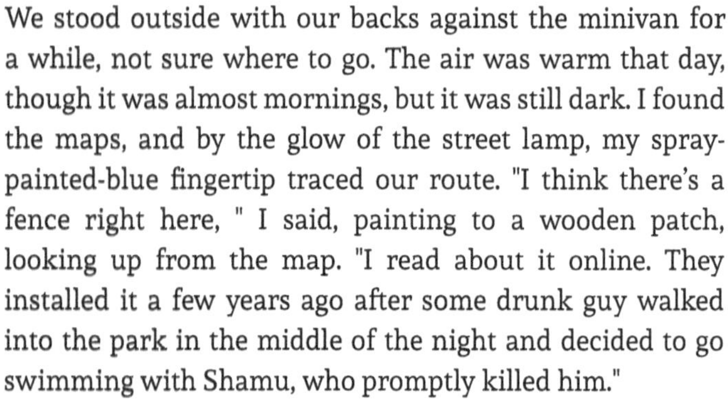

We stood outside with our backs against the minivan for a while, not sure where to go. The air was warm that day, though it was almost mornings, but it was still dark. I found the maps, and by the glow of the street lamp, my spray-painted-blue fingertip traced our route. "I think there's a fence right here, " I said, painting to a wooden patch, looking up from the map. "I read about it online. They installed it a few years ago after some drunk guy walked into the park in the middle of the night and decided to go swimming with Shamu, who promptly killed him."

"Seriously? "

"Yeah, so if a guy can make it in drunk, surely we can make it in sober. I mean, we're ninjas. "

"Well, maybe you're a ninja, " he said.

"You're just a really loud awkward ninja, " I said. "But we're both ninjas. "

I tucked my hair behind my ears, pulled my hood up and scrunched it with the strings.

"Okay, " I said, "memorize the map."

Sea World was shaped like a triangle. And I'd plotted some places which we had to travel through. One side of the theme park was a road, which was regularly patrolled by the night watchmen. The second side was a lake, like, a mile around. The third side had a drainage ditch. And where there water-filled drains near lakes, there are alligators.

I grabbed Quentin by both of his shoulders and turned him toward me. "We're going to get caught, probably, and when we do, just let me talk. You just look caught and be that weird mix of innocent and confident, and we'll be fine."

He looked the car and patted his brown puffy hair, and said, under his breath, "I'm a ninja."

"Damned right you are! Now let's go." And we jogged across 1-Drive and then bushwhacked through the thicket of oak trees, my arms making the way for me, pushing aside the bushes as we walked toward the moat. Finally we were out of the trees and there was a parkway on our right and the moat straight ahead of us. We took off running through the bushes and I, then, made a sharp turn toward the parkway. "Now, now!" I said, and he followed across the six lanes of highway.

We made it across and knelt on the grass for a few seconds. Then I pointed to the strip of trees between Sea World's huge parking lot and the still black water of the moat. We ran along that line of trees, Q in front of me. Then I pulled the back of his T-shirt and said quietly, almost whispered, "Now the moat."

"Ladies first," he said.

"No really, be my guest."

He ran in the disgusting layer of brackish algae, and jumped into waist deep water and then high-stepped across. The water really stank. I jumped in, splashing all the water all over Q. he turned around and splashed me.

"Ninjas don't splash other ninjas," I said.

"The true ninja doesn't make a splash at all," he said.

"Oh touché."

EIGHTEEN

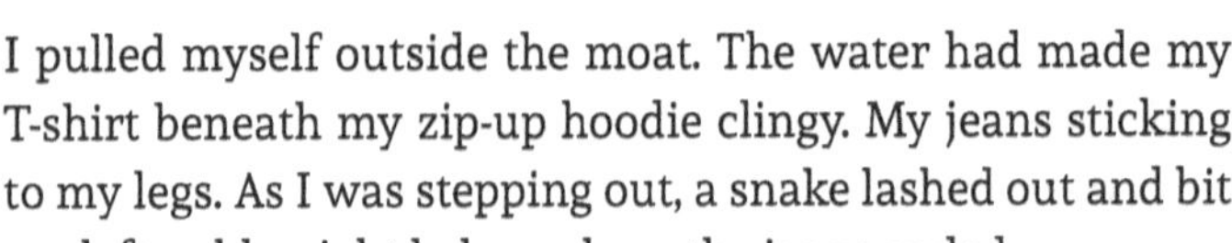

I pulled myself outside the moat. The water had made my
T-shirt beneath my zip-up hoodie clingy. My jeans sticking
to my legs. As I was stepping out, a snake lashed out and bit
my left ankle, right below where the jeans ended.

"Shit," I said, and looked down at it, "Shit." The snake still
clinging to my ankle. Q dove down and grabbed the snake
by it's tail and ripped it from my leg and threw it back into
the black water. "Ow, god," I said, it really hurt, "What was
it? Was it a moccasin?"

"I don't know. Lie down, lie down." He then took my leg
in his hands, and pulled up my jeans. Two drop of blood
coming out, where the fangs had been. He leaned down and
put his mouth on the wound and sucked, trying to draw
out the venom. He spit, and was going to go back to my leg
when I said, "Wait, I see it." He got terrified and jumped up.
"No, no. It's just a garter snake." I pointed into the moat, to a
little garter snake skirting on the surface. From a luminous
distance, the thing didn't look much scarier than a baby
lizard.

"Thank god," he sighed. Sitting down, beside me.

The bleeding had already stopped. "How was making out
with my leg?" I laughed.

"Pretty good," he said, I leaned myself into him a little.
My left arm touching his chest, I could feel his ribs against

my bony shoulder.

"I shaved this morning for precisely this reason. I was like, 'well, you never know when someone's going to clamp down on your calf and try to suck out the snake poison.'"

There was a six-feet tall chain-link fence before us. "Honestly, first the garter snakes and now this fence? This security is sort of insulting for a ninja." I said. I scrabbled up, swung myself and climbed down like a ladder. He came behind me.

We, then, ran through briar patch and we came out to an asphalt path. The little speakers playing soft Muzak. Maybe to keep the animals calm.

"Margo," he said, with a hint of excitement in his voice, "We made it to the Sea World."

"Seriously," I said, and jogged away. He followed. I stopped at a seal tank, but there was not even a single seal inside.

"Margo," he said again, "We're in the Sea World."

"Enjoy it," I said, as quietly as I could, "'cause here comes the security."

He started to run but watching me stand still, he stopped.

A guy sauntered up wearing a SeaWorld security vest and asked us casually, "How y'all?" he was holding a can of something in his hand.

"We were just on our way out, actually," I said.

"Well, that's certain," he said. "The question is whether we were walking out or getting driven out by the Orange County sheriff."

"If it's all the same to you," I said. "We'd rather walk."

The man laughed. "You know a man got knilt here a couple of years ago jumping in the big tank, and they told us we canin't never let anybody go if they break in, no matter if they're pretty."

"Well, then I guess you have to arrest us."

"But that's the thing. I'm 'bout to get off and go home and have a beer and get some sleep, if I call the police they'll take their sweet time in coming. I'm just thinkin' out loud here," he said.

I wiggled into my wet pocket, and pulled out a moat-water-soaked hundred-dollar bill.

"Well, y'all best be getting on now. If I were you, I wouldn't walk out past the whale tank. It's got all-night security cameras all 'round it, and we wouldn't want anyone to know y'all was here." the guard said.

"Yessir," I said, and walked off the darkness with the guard. "Man," I said as he went away, "I really didn't want to pay that perv. But, oh well. Money's for spendin'"

"Thank god, he's not turning us in," Q said. I didn't say anything.

NINETEEN

I was staring at something past him, "I felt this exact same way when I got into Universal Studios," I said after a moment. "It's kind of cool and everything, but there's nothing much to see. The rides aren't working. Everything cool is locked up. Most animals are put into different tanks at night." I turned around, just gazing at the place we just broke into. "I guess the pleasure isn't in being inside."

"What's the pleasure?" he asked.

"Planning, I guess. I don't know. Doing stuff never feels as good as you hope it'll feel."

"This feels pretty good to me," he confessed. "Even if there isn't anything to see."

He sat on a park bench, I sat beside him. We were staring at the sea tank before us, an empty sea tank. It contained no seals, just an unoccupied island with rocky outcroppings made of plastic. I was tired. My head on his shoulder, facing him, and maybe I could feel him breathe against my forehead, and maybe we could stay there until morning. When people would walk past us, thinking we were tourists too and we'd disappear into them. Except, I didn't want to disappear into the crowd and I didn't have time till morning.

"Q," I said. And he turned to look at me. He was half-asleep, but then realised why I took his name. The Muzak on the speakers had been turned up, only it wasn't anymore – it was real music. The old, jazzy song 'Stars Fell on Alabama'.

I stood up. Q stood up and reached his hand and said, "May I have this dance?"

His green green eyes and his blue jeans sticking to his legs from the moat water. I gave him my hand, "You may." Then his hand was on my waist, mine on his shoulder. And then step-step-sidestep, step-step-sidestep. We fox-trotted all the way along the seal tank, and still the song went on about the falling stars. "Sixth-grade slow dance," I said, and we switched positions. My hands on his shoulders and his on my hips, elbows locked, two feet between us. And we fox-trotted some more, until the song ended. He dipped me, just how they taught at the Crown School of Dance. I raised one leg and gave him all the weight as he dipped me. I trusted him.

TWENTY

We went to 7-Eleven on 1-Drive and bought dish towels, and tried to wash the slime and stink from the moat water off our clothes and skin. He filled up the gas tank to where it had been before our drive to Orlando. We didn't pass through any interstates on our way back home. Quentin and I were surfing through the radio stations, trying to figure out which one of then was playing 'Stars fell on Alabama,' but I turned it down and said, "All in all, I think it was a success."

"Absolutely," he said, "I do wonder if it'll be different tomorrow."

"Yeah," I said, "me too." I left it hanging in the air. I *knew* it's going to be different, at least for me. Even for Quentin, because of Chuck's one eyebrow gone and everything. But for me, it was going to be entirely different. Not because of the rain I brought down on people, but because my plan hasn't ended yet. "Hey, speaking of tomorrow, as a thanks for your hard work and dedication on this remarkable evening, I would like to give you a small present." I dug around beneath my feet and pulled out a digital camera. "Take it," I said. "And use the power of the Tinky Winky wisely."

He laughed and put the camera in his pocket. "I'll download the picture when I get home and give it to you at school?"

I know he was expecting a better reply, but I just said, "Yeah, or whatever." I shrugged.

We turned into Jefferson Park. It was 5:42. We drove down Jefferson Drive to Jefferson Court and then turned onto our road, Jefferson Way. No one said anything, we filled the 7-Eleven bag with trash trying to make the minivan look it was in the garage since the last six hours. In the other bag, I gave him the Vaseline, spray paint, and the last full Mountain Dew.

He was walking towards his house, me standing there silently. He paused, with bags in both his hand, he turned and stared at me. "Well, it was a hell of a night," he finally said.

"Come here," I said, and he took a step forward. I hugged him the bags made it difficult for him to hug me, but he couldn't drop them either. I was on my tiptoes and my mouth against his ear, and said, very clearly, "I. Will. Miss. Hanging. Out. With. You."

"You don't have to," he said.

"If you don't like them anymore," he said, "just hang out with me. My friends are actually, like, nice."

I smiled , "I'm afraid it's not possible," I whispered and let him go, but kept looking at him, taking step by step backward. He raised his eyebrows and smiled, I smiled back. And he went inside the unlocked front door.

I climbed up a tree and then went on the roof outside my bedroom window. I unlatched the window and crawled inside.

TWENTY-ONE

It was time for the next step of my plan. When I went inside my room, I saw Ruthie sleeping. I tried to do everything as silently as I could, not to wake her up. I changed my stinky clothes into a fresh pair of jeans and a T-shirt. And picked my bag, and kept all the things I'll be needing for the rest of the time. Along with my map, flashlight, and my car keys (yes, I had an extra pair of those in my room, I lied to Quentin just so I could go along with him.) and some other supplies. I had to leave before anybody in the street could wake. It was 6:27 in the morning. My parents would've woken up already, I didn't have time to check up on them.

So without any second thoughts, I snuck out again. I tried to push my car as silently as I could, not to wake up people. I didn't switch it on until I was four blocks away from my house. I, then, realised it didn't have any gas and where I had to go was too far to run on this amount of gas.

I went straight to Wal-mart to buy the rest of the supplies I'll need, along with some food. The guy, who we ran into at night was still there.

"Hey," he said.

"Hey, I thought you got off at one," I said.

"Um, yeah. I-uh, had too," he stuttered, I was looking at the aisle beside him, "but...hm, long story."

I started to regret asking the question, and I was looking through the food counter, thinking what I could get which will last for a few days. "My mum called me for some work, so I had to get my car.." He was still talking. But I had no interest in the work his mum gave him. But since I'd asked him, I couldn't cut him off too. So, I pretend to listen to his whole story.

"Well, at least you'll get paid for your extra shift," I said.

"Uh-huh, and the best part is..." he went on. I really needed to get out. I couldn't afford to waste anymore time there, and if he kept talking, my head will explode. Well, I don't blame him too, I was the sleep-deprived-teen-annoyed-with-everything, I picked some stuff and kept it on his counter, "I'll take these." I paid the bill and got going. "Hope to see you again," he said.

"Bye." And I took off to the gas station.

My next stop was this other place, where I was going to stay for the next two days. I avoided to go from places I could expect people for school, or anywhere for that matter. I got inside the car and turned on the radio. It was playing 'Stars Fell on Alabama', I smiled and continued to drive.

I looked around, and thought to myself, this is probably the last time I'm looking at these places, these faces, or even driving through these roads.

It was not that long of a drive. And in an hour, the place stood before me. I got off the car. There it was. I was a little overwhelmed with excitement, how everything's going to be different now – How I can be whoever I want to be, no more sneaking out. I can create a life of my own now.

"And so it begins." I said to myself, "a new chapter of my life."

About The Author

Vartika Vashista is a budding author living in New Delhi, who is here with a young adult fan fiction. She is someone who's a believer of creativity and always up for new experiences ahead.